KIKI RETURNS TO SCHOOL

The Importance of Education

Esther Ugezene

Published by:
Professional Publishing House
1425 W. Manchester Ave., Ste. B
Los Angeles, CA 90047
(323) 750-3592
professionalpublishinghouse@yahoo.com
www.professionalpublishinghouse.com

First Printing February, 2023

ISBN 978-1-7328982-5-7

Table of Contents

Acknowledgments

I give thanks to God and His Son Jesus.

To me, the author of the book, for the relentless effort I made writing the book.

I convey my regards to:

Mr. Stephen Ugezene(Engineer)

Mr. Alexander Ugezene

Ms. Anthonia Ugezene

Lt. Ngezelonye V. Ugezene

Lt. Augustina Ogwu (nee-Ugezene)

Lt. Anna Ugezene.

To my uncles, aunties, cousins, nieces, and nephews. To my early school days mates like Pastor John Odor, Kennedy Uzoka, Dennis Wogu, Ndubuisi Anumenechi, Chiedu Dibigbo, and Nwaenu Aniemeke.

I choose to pass my regards also to Onitsha-Ugbo Village and its native children, the children of ezechime and members of Onitsha-Ugbo Development and Cultural Foundation(ODCF).

Last but not the least, I thank my loving father, Ugezene Okwuonne and my mother Nwaewunashi Catherine Ugezene for, more importantly, their encouragement.

About the Author

Esther Ugezene grew up in the United States, which she says is the best place in the world. Esther holds a B.S. degree in Healthcare (with a pharm option) from Scantron School of Correspondence. She attended California State University Dominquez Hills, Carson, California, where she studied Medical Laboratory and Science Technology. She completed her laboratory work through C.M.E. Resource DE under the supervision of Ann Frees. Esther graduated from Cal. State Dominquez Hills as an honor student. She received the California Community Honor Award in 1994. She was an active member of Alpha Gamma Sigma.

Esther graduated from Asaba Girls Grammar School in Nigeria. During her fourth year of high school, she was elected as the water prefect of the school. And she was a member and secretary of the liberally and debating society.

Esther was the secretary of the students community meetings in her Village Quarters. As a young child, she was selected secretary of the Catholic Church Youth Association.

Esther's work experience includes working in the medical field and in education. She has worked many years in the pharmacy department at hospitals, and as an on-call nurse. She tutored for two and half years in area of chemistry, algebra, biology, English and general psychology in the Community College.

Introduction

This book, *Kiki Returns to School* is written to make readers have a clear understanding of the importance of education. It is written in details and apart from centering the text on KiKi, it goes as far as touching on areas that exposes an interested reader to the knowledge of different available professions. If you put your interest and focus on reading the book, you will be well enlightened and will be able to make some necessary decisions on which choice of field to follow as regards to having your degree.

The book helps one to further acknowledge why one should deem it absolutely necessary not to take things for granted. Your future must be seriously considered in your youthful days. In this wise, it does help to avoid the thought of, "Had I known. . ."

Chapter One

As an intelligent person with an outgoing character and personality, Kiki remained determined. She did not give up on wanting to succeed. After all, she realized how most of her age-mates graduated from high school before her, even if she was more intelligent than them. Following her disappointments, she had come to the ground where she resolved to cling to the saying: *A determination to bridge the gap.* Because of her hard experience, she had, in no time, become more mature.

Having a baby out of an unwanted pregnancy was not an easy experience. After she had her baby boy named Henry Junior, she took the rest of her high school classes without further delay, enabling her to receive the General Education Development Certificate (GED), which was equivalent to a high school diploma. With a zeal to focus on schooling and receive her university degree before thirty-five years old, she made a strong resolution and held onto it, vowing not to be a fool at forty.

Although Kiki might be young, she could make good and sound decisions, and she was hardworking. These were some attributes she had as an intelligent person. Her strong power of positive thinking carried her through a lot of times. Her intelligent quotient ranked toward 100%. As a positive thinker, she liked nothing that would drag her into negative visions. As she accepted the importance of education, she took "no" as the answer that she would not give up.

The importance of education stemmed from achievement or success. With the acquisition of education, rewarding opportunities await. With the completion of school or education and holding on to a good job, your living standard improved. Getting a rewarding job after completing school could elevate your financial status. With a more lucrative or better-paying job, someone like Kiki realized she could own a house and a car(s) of her own.

Having abilities to put her thoughts into perspective, Kiki often marveled over how engineering worked in building bridges, houses, and rails. She wondered what it took to become a qualified engineer. The calculations and physics involved the mathematics behind the calculations of densities and fortification of walls. With curiosity and research, she learned of degree-oriented professions with the completion of university education. Professions like engineering, medicine, law, and many others had long been available. With four years of university, she could earn her degree in engineering.

Kiki's son's father, Henry Senior, after graduating from college, went further into his education. He kept working for a bank until he advanced to a bank manager. He continued to be well off. HOPE, it is said, does not falter. Kiki hoped that someday she would rekindle her love affair with Henry and they would be married. During the time she was reading for her GED certificate, she had a friend named Trina Laurel. Trina became a certified nursing assistant and was interested in pursuing a nursing career. Her ultimate goal was to hold a Bachelor of Science in Nursing (BSN), and this was what she would do to become successful.

Kiki's area of interest was to become a sociologist, so she was going to study sociology. Earning her degree would entail living up to a higher standard. A qualified graduate who got a job could have a starting annual salary of $48,000. 00. Readers, I encourage you to research the starting salaries of graduates of higher institutes of learning.

After Kiki had received her general education certificate, she started her university career. This time, her son was already in grade school. Even if she had him out of wedlock, she promised herself not to live on regrets anymore. Although despite the promise, she still could not help feeling ashamed of not meeting expectations like most of her early school-age mates did. While she was at university, she continued to work. This time she was working at the college as a tutor. She maintained high marks and received scholarships. Her grade point average was always close to 4.0. In addition to her earnings from work and scholarships, she was also receiving academic grants. So, with the way she structured her plans, she could care for herself and her child.

Chapter Two

Even because of Kiki's grade point average, she received a scholarship after her second year semester to travel to London and study one year of educational credential courses. The school promised that after her graduation, with the one-year credential attached to her major degree, she would receive instant employment. The school would give her the job. However, she chose to suspend the offer. She preferred to travel for the course after her graduation. Luckily, the scholarship award board accepted her request. She knew she would eventually use the scholarship award, but for her, going to London would give her new and different insights.

Meanwhile, at the University, where she was an honors student and belonged to the

Dean's list and meeting every quarter, she normally received the conduct of excellent performance from the student office of academic talent. Several tangible awards followed with the dean's list roster. The impression always made her outstandingly elated. It indeed let her look on the brighter side. She registered and belonged to the meeting of the honorary award group. They held meetings held every Friday in the evenings. With the way they organized it, the members paid a paltry sum of money. The money, at the end of the year, was used to send off the predecessors. The rest remained in the safe by the successors for future needs. Kiki counted herself blessed or lucky to belong to the dean's list. The highest point to maintain as an honor student was 4.00 G.P.A Some students had 3.5 and above, and they made up the list with Kiki. An honor student had more advantages over someone with below 3.00 G.P.A For a student to maintain 3.00 G.P.A. or above, he/she was above average.

The dean's organization had different functioning positions. Examples were the position of president, treasurer, door attendant, secretary, public relations, and others. The post given to Kiki in the meeting was public relations officer. Her responsibility was to distribute fliers for the organization during times of events. She reached out to the public more effectively for the dean's meetings.

Also, she notified the members of their monthly monetary contributions. She usually worked closely with the secretary who documented her gathered information afterward. So, with having to put herself in school, everything was working out with promises and progress. Apart from the feeling of enhancement she enjoyed as a "PRO," she was also glad to find herself in a position of leadership and authority.

Kiki's admiration for Cherry, her early school friend, was heightened, especially after she saw how she was moving on progressively. She had also come to learn that putting your faith, hope, and trust in God is very advantageous. Since she was aware that Cherry was a strong Christian, she too converted to Christianity, whereby she attended church regularly and prayed to God in Jesus' name. Her understanding of discipline emanated from parental upbringing and education, but also, she learned discipline could be taught through reading, praying, and practicing the ways of God. The Ten Commandments—the biblical law of Moses—were part of her best readings in the book. The Ten Commandments were great ways to teach discipline. Apparently, good and honest ways of life that we have learned to live were also by adherence to the teachings of Christianity and education. There were some numbers of Christian schools, educating the societies, communities, and the likes of the right and expected outcomes in life. Because of having a good Christian background, and like the saying: "Slow and steady wins the race," Cherry was always steady and stable. Even though Cherry was somewhat passive, her steadiness and ability to listen and follow instructions helped her tremendously.

Education, with its various important tools, had been what most humans fancied or admired. In the struggle to be educated, some could not meet up to expected grades. However, with persistence and perseverance, they had a breakthrough. It is said, "Practice makes perfect."Most steps to achievement had been cultured into having education or higher education, and part of the reason was to make improvements through development, a better outlook, and living up to the right standard. Having the right education also helped to mold humans into the right behavior.

Much that Kiki was aware that the father of his son became a bank manager, she kept her hope alive. One afternoon, somewhere near a park, her car tire went flat, and while she was trying to pump it, surprisingly, the person standing there, who stopped to help her, was Henry Senior. Immediately, she saw him; she was perplexed.

I am the author of the book *Kiki The School Truant*. I recommend you read it. Note the two approaches both Kiki and Cherry, her early childhood school friend, had about education. From *Kiki Returns to School*, one can understand how Kiki made it. As was mentioned earlier, her intelligence and outstanding character carried her through.

Chapter Three

Obviously, education with various University majors had been a strong foundation. Kiki had applied her thinking and deduced that for someone to become somebody in instances of qualifications, he/she must be educated. Even only for the need for knowledge through education, there was a high attraction of foreigners to overseas. They traveled to countries like the United Kingdom, the United States, and others that had better and more opportunities for education as they want to fill the gap.

A qualified person, after receiving a degree, would start a well-paid job, whereby his life began to have a different outlook or view. His position became prestigious since he had to be molded into such behavior that entailed his ways. His conduct in society became more remarkable and acceptable. A medical doctor's annual income exceeded

$85,000. 00. The cure and healing a doctor gave to a patient were usually effective because of being highly educated.

Before Yolanda Andrew became a nurse practitioner, she decided with her intuition to show an exemplary life. After her high school graduation, she decided she would combine working and schooling. She began her goal by putting herself into licensed vocational nursing (LVN) training. After passing her licensure examination and obtaining a job as an LVN, her income margin was pushed up. You know what?She did not stop there. While working, she started taking some general courses that would lead her to enter the training to be a registered nurse. After she had completed the requirements, she was admitted into the registered nursing program. Subsequently, she graduated and became a holder of an Associate of Science degree in nursing, and her earning income was raised at the hospital where she worked.

With the accomplishment so far, Yolanda's next move was to study further and become a Bachelor of Science in nursing degree holder. Thereafter, she would go for the master of nursing and study to the level of a nurse practitioner. With that position, she can prescribe medications. With positive motives, goals, and sound decisions, Yolanda knows that she would live a better and more comfortable life. So, she used this quote: "Always have self-confidence, set your goals, and make decisions without doubts."

Abigail Fieldman became a linguist after experiencing how complicated communication was when two or more people do not understand themselves because of the different nativity. So, after high school, she studied language at the University.

Even then, with all that education provided that was not mentioned here, there was great joy in facing the routine. Note this short poetic song about schooling:

THERE IS A WAY, GO TO SCHOOL
There is a way,
go to school,
go to school,
go to school

There is a way,
go to school,
go to school,
go to school
Early in the morning.

There is a way,
brush your teeth,
brush your teeth,
brush your teeth

There is a way,
brush your teeth,
brush your teeth,
brush your teeth
Early in the morning.

There is a way,
clean your shoe,
clean your shoe,
clean your shoe

There is a way,
clean your shoe,
clean your shoe,
clean your shoe
Early in the morning.

A waking up hour of 6:00 a.m. in the mornings prepared a student's mind for a class starting at 8:00 a.m. At an early age, it applied, too. Classes usually began at 8:00 a.m. and before 3:30 p.m., they are over. After a teacher must have taught up to three or four subjects, he then sent the pupils out to play. They played a variety of games, from running around to hide and seek games, and other spot games. The fields were wide enough to throw balls. Different games like basketball, football, and tennis are practiced. After an hour-long, the students were ready to get in and continue with their class lessons. There were numerous subjects and classes to study, starting with English,mathematics, history, and the rest. All stems to boost the knowledge of an interested, hardworking, and bright student. Note these outstanding and exceptional qualities of an educated person:

1) An educated person has a great deal of discipline.

2) An educated person carries himself with a high respect and orderly presentation.

3) To have an education means you are painstaking and can comport yourself.

4) An educated person can accept challenges

5) The importance of education adds up to being able to reap greater rewards in your accomplishment.

6) Having a good education is the acquisition of the ability to advance consistently in life.

7) Having an education is the ability to go further and be trained in higher institutes or universities.

8) Education provides the means to build big houses or bridges for fortification.

9) Education provides the means to embark on health care research to cure severe sicknesses.

10) Education gives room to studying foreign languages to combat language barriers.

Chapter Four

It is essential to note that it takes the fact that Kiki had a high intelligent quotient (IQ) and this was the reason she made her success, too. She grasped and understood lessons faster than most of her folks. She truly possessed the qualities of a very intelligent person in nature. Above everything else, she could make concrete decisions. The reason behind her decision to continue with schooling resulted from having thought or reasoned that education was very important in life. She remained the person whose character and disposition continued to carry her through. Even as a child, she had always possessed that positive mind and an outgoing personality. She was good at exploring the world and the environment.

When Kiki had an unwanted pregnancy, she did not resolve to have an abortion. Instead, she deemed it right not to allow such action to hurt her for the rest of her life. At that young age of her delinquency, when her father sent her away by refusing her accommodation, she got a job which she did for fourteen years. As a reflection of her, most of the things she did was applying her intelligence to make important decisions. So, having learned some hard lessons, raising her child in a severe fix, she decided successful yields would justify the means.

Now and then she ran into the father of her child, whom she was aware was living comfortably and had not married. Even then, they became fond of having a few moments of chat. They appeared to still have some hidden interests in each other, although it was hard to understand and express it.

From the area of wisdom, Kiki focused and followed the ways of education and swore to never repeat the same mistake. So she placed her son in school and made sure he would not be a school truant. Her son, Henry Junior, becomes exceptionally intelligent and never repeated in any school year. He informed Kiki, his mother, that he was going to study history at University when he grew up. He said that he would work in the Library as an administrator. He liked and appreciated history because it was for the study of keeping records.

One could perceive that with the way Kiki was waiting and pursuing her goals, she was praying and wishing that Henry Senior asked for her hand in marriage. For he also has that reservation, especially as he could see their son growing up to be a reasonable person. Conversations ensued between Kiki and her son's father at their encounters. Then she came to realize that he was apprehensive. He seemed to feel that he only disappointed Kiki by denying his son. He was aware of how highly intelligent Kiki was, and her zeal and strong determination for a more positive change were amazing to him.

The things worthy of doing for Kiki that were denied her by her parents for not meeting expectations made her feel down sometimes. For example, when it was time to give her gifts, they could not deprive her.

As she continued to follow the right path, she contemplated that in the future, once she did that lucrative job, she would buy a five-bedroom home and a BMW car. She hoped that in the future she would own a daycare school to teach children preschool and kindergarten education.

Much that she was aware of, she knew that the silver anniversary of marking the marriage ceremony was twenty-five years, and the golden anniversary of marriage was fifty years. She wanted to count herself lucky after marriage when she eventually does, especially if it was Henry Senior, her son's father. With those future desires thrilling her heart, she could not wait to fulfill them.

So, while she suspended going to study for an additional educational credential award given to her, she then graduated in sociology first. She was fortunate enough that the scholarship award-giving office agreed to hold the offer on her behalf.

During the season of her graduation, she was elated to hear from Henry Senior that he was interested in her and wanted them both to start their love affair all over again. He even said that he would like to marry her, especially now that she became a graduate. He had more work as a bank manager, and he was studying to receive a master's degree. Virtually everything that would add up to progress, Kiki and him had pursued in recent development. He had rekindled the passion he had for her. Then, with more hope, Kiki remained with strong determinations.

Since her interest in owning a daycare school remained fresh, she always had enchantment in her heart that went this way:

WHERE ARE THE FLOWER GOWNS:

Where are the flowers gowns
Sunshine passage
Where are the flowers gowns
 Long time ago
 Where are the flowers gowns
 Young girls pick them
When will they ever learn (x2)

Where're the young girls gone
Sunshine passage
Where are the young girls gone
 Longtime ago
'Where're the young girls gone
Gone to young men
When will they ever learn
When will they ever learn

Where are the young men gone
Sunshine passage
Where are the young men gone
Long time ago
Where are the young men gone

Gone to soldiers
When will they ever learn
When will they ever learn

Chapter Five

Kiki continued to pursue her goals, and she usually came out accomplished afterward. As she decided to go abroad to London to study the educational credential course, the financial aid board did not hesitate to reason with her. She had an outstanding academic standing with the school. Besides, she knew there would be more doors of opportunities to open for her in the future, especially when she considered going for a master's degree. That would be when she returned to the United States. She expected to explore what she deemed to be a different world abroad. It would also enable her to experience another world.

After receiving her degree in sociology, she left the United States for London. She arrived at the campus of the University on Saturday where the gateman took her straight to the dormitory, and she was glad to join the dormitory inmates. On Monday, after the students' lectures were over, someone from the office of student affairs introduced Kiki to her fellow students on campus. With them exchanging some pleasantries, they created magic moments of the time. Then, subsequently, as the weekdays went by, they all got their mind fixed on their classes.

Taking fast-paced classes helped her focus and complete the one-year course within the year. The University in the United States kept her on track. Every semester, the office of financial aid was sending her an educational check. As she completed the course, she returned to the States. She submitted a copy of the one-year educational certificate with her degree to the office of graduation and the admission and records. Having met the University requirements, she was invited to the student service office.

She received many packages with job offers, and from there, she had to find what her options were as far as deciding to teach classes in social studies. Later, after sorting herself out, she accepted two days part-time working for the school in the evenings and Monday through Thursday, working for the post office as a supervisor. She was making a good salary and filled with satisfaction.

Kiki's son, Henry Junior, becomes a University graduate and a librarian. He had taken time to read through the accomplishment of some great and notable individuals. He became much too aware of what it took, for example, a great country like the United States of America to elect a president. Part of the requirements is that the USA president must be well-learned. At least, have a university education. His determination and interest in leading should emanate from learnable knowledge. Through implementation based on integrity, hard work, and discipline, he must be ready to prove himself. Some presidents received degrees in dual majors. In some instances, a president received his degree in political science and a second degree as an attorney. Before being elected as president, he might have become a man of high integrity and honor. Like Kiki, her son, Henry, had taken much fancy to the achieved and successful ones that he marveled over the steps it took being termed the learned.

To learn how to read and write, a person must be ready to be educated, otherwise, he might continue to feel or behave dumb in the midst. When most parents decided to send their kids to early schools, they understood that they had concrete objectives. It took at least the age of four or five for a child who was in school to put words down in writing. Close to the same age, he focused on written words which his senses registered in the brain. Apparently, it was very important to register a child for early age education. This was so important because you would not want the child to miss out enough to become misinformed or confused. If a child began school at a given or an expected age, there should not be refusal or disappointment from the school authorities that is late. So in this wise, "Make hay while the sun shines for time and tide wait for no man."

Read this: Xyda Mandy was a stay-at-home mother who failed her two sons and did not feel that putting them through school was necessary. Mr. Felix Mandy, her husband and the father of her two sons, Alex Mandy and Andrew Mandy, worked in a laundromat and earned a meager amount of salary.

Instead of Xyda seeking educational assistance, she was too proud and reluctant. She remained static and let the two kids skip pre-school and kindergarten education. The sad aspect was that English was not their first language and while she sat at home, she only communicated with them in their native language, which was from Africa. Eventually, as those children were growing up and their mother seemed to be a know-it-all whose best interest was to leave the children uneducated. The fact was that she was ignorant and incorrigible. Her lack of interest in even learning how to read and write resulted in a lack of insight and foresight.

By mere intentions, she watched both kids pass early age and did not place them in school. At their fifth age, she blatantly said that they should wait until later to begin. The bitter aspect was that she refused to inquire about someone who knew better. Even when she listened to the television, she did not comprehend. Funny enough, her two sons knew how to speak their African language, but have great difficulty with the English language.

As time passed by, Xyda, instead of buckling up to change her stubborn attitude, convinced her husband to send the two boys home to her husband's grandmother. Mr. Mandy somewhat perceived that such an action could compound some problems for them in the future. However, he was passive. Later, as he reached the Village, he acted according to his intuition. First, he felt it better to let go of what seemed to the children being "tied to their mother's apron's string," or an undue attachment to their mother. Mr. Mandy decided the transition might be for the betterment. So, when they got to the Village, he arranged for one of his cousins to see that Alex and Andrew eventually start school that year, although this time they were already nine and seven years old, respectively. At the end, he returned to the city in the states, ignoring his wife.

Chapter Six

In terms of the progression that led Bryant Don to own a small-scale business at twenty-five years old, the strategy was that after he graduated at eighteen years old from high school, he received his high school diploma and started working. While working, he took a loan that a financial company offered to him. In addition, he bought a small business store. Then afterward, he started working in his business and remained the owner and manager. To enable him to run his store more closely, he had to quit his present job. Meanwhile, after a couple of years, he paid off the loan. To become an expert and hopefully form the business into a corporation in the future, he attended University. He registered for part-time classes and continued to work full time in his business. His major course of study was business administration. He usually expressed that he loved further education because he knew its value. He aimed to advance toward a doctorate (Ph. D.) in later years.

As Kiki held the position of the post office as supervisor, she usually closed at 3:00 p.m. Then, on Thursdays and Fridays, she lectured part-time in the school. With her savings, she makes a down payment for a five-bedroom home. The negotiation for the home was on a twenty-five-year mortgage payment. However, she planned to complete payment between fifteen to twenty years' time duration. She also kept the two-bedroom house she inherited from her parents. Since she was making up her mind to settle down in marriage, she envisioned having two more children. As she secured her parents' house, she renovated it. She wanted to leave it as a family house and also to use it to keep the memory of her parents.

By the time Lewis Arkson started school at five years of age in the city of Goldfield, New Jersey, he was making poor grades. With his poor performances, when he reached junior high, he had to repeat. As time proceeded, he barely made it. He repeated the eleventh grade and could not complete the twelfth-grade level. After the nineteenth year, his parents were advised to register him with Career and Adult Education where he could study and receive the GED. He began the GED classes rather reluctantly, with a nonchalant spirit. However, he struggled really hard and made himself believe this statement of fact: "The struggle continues."So with perseverance, Lewis passed and received the GED certificate. He was overjoyed, and with the light in his eye, he did not want to give up his determination to go further with schooling. He then enrolled in University. His major course of study was education. He would, after passing the C-BEST examination, teach history. Covering the college courses, he received financial aid, which made him appreciate more and also not give up. Following that, he took an educational loan, which he reserved until he needed it.

While many individuals have realized or experienced the high benefits education offers, many more, even those who cannot attain or afford to become educated, fancy its roots and benefits deeply. Even in life, in part, attaining the SELF-ACTUALIZATION level of Maslow's Theory is important in reaching a high degree of satisfaction in life. For example, realizing that at five years of age, one is ready to start schooling marks a beginning to life fulfillment. Taking accomplishment stage by stage, attainable levels of self-actualization really gives fullness thereafter. During the eighteenth year of completing your secondary or high school graduation means an accomplishment stage that prepares you for the world. There is a high degree of happiness following the initial stage. With the present level of maturity and accomplishment, the option may be to acquire a job while you either take time or start soon to advance in your educational pursuit, which of course means to enroll in the University. The four years it would take you to graduate from the University also means an additional level of fulfillment. This once more brings you to a new level of self-actualization. It then makes you feel that you are somebody and not a know-nothing kind of person who has little or no self-worth.

Poem:

Education or schooling is sweet but learning may be hard.

There a child is running to school with his bag.

Then the parents' smile.

Such a smile even leads them to laughter, ha-ha.

Mr. Alfred Hughes realized somewhere in the course of his life that the need to have a qualification was beneficial. He knew how much he missed out by not having a high school diploma. The work Alfred did that helped him earn a living was labor. He worked on a contract as a painter. Even if he was meeting up financially, he wanted to have a change.

He loved the nursing profession and wanted to become a registered nurse. He made some inquiries into nursing. He found out that his high school diploma was required. So he went back to school at twenty-five years of age. He received the equivalency of a high school diploma. Then he enrolled in a college after meeting up with other requirements of admission into the college. He began by completing the nursing prerequisites.

Then, after one semester of being on the waiting list, he was accepted into the registered nursing program. After two years, he completed the nursing courses and was qualified to take the board examination, whereby he would receive his license to practice as a registered nurse. You can see that Alfred went back to school because he was not satisfied working as a painter. He wanted something more professional, and he definitely got it.

Another fascinating hint was about Mr. Howard Abel. When Mr. Howard Abel's fortune knocked at his door, he was ready to embrace it, but it required having a first degree in television production. His goal was to become a television producer and one of the television personalities. He wanted his dream of owning a television network to manifest into reality. So after his graduation, he began working by appearing and acting in different movies. Then he became very rich and could buy the network and its TV channel. Furthermore, as a successful owner of the TV channel, he sold some show hours to entertainers and movie casters. He had that going on while he earned a large income as a movie actor. One can carefully see that he was really successful in advancing in education. You see, this book does not only focus on Kiki's returning to school but also touches on other interested individuals who appreciate education.

After watching the movie about how this Nigerian actress named Genevieve Nnaji became famous, no one would hesitate to consider education as a most valuable treasure. In the movie, Genevieve is a law student. She possessed a tough personality of a disciplined person. Besides, she came from a highly disciplined home. Her parents were educated. Although her father had retired, he could still sponsor her law school education. Fortunately, because of Genevieve's zeal and determination, she left no stone unturned in her academic pursuit. She never wanted to mess around. Even if she had a male friend, they hardly had time to visit each other. Of course, that was what she wanted for the time being. To her, having an opposite relationship and spending time should wait. She had many responsible and well-educated suitors coming to ask for her hands in marriage. Even then, it did not matter to them if they helped her complete the law profession financially. Those suitors were desperate for her. It was a competition among them to see who would win her. However, despite their approaches, she rejected them. She explained that unless she had completed her course, she would consider one of the suitors. As we can note, she was letting faith and confidence stay firm in the way. With this, just read and absorb this quote:"Let faith, hope, and determination be the main keys to the pursuit of your goal." Genevieve goes as far as rejecting one of them who was a very wealthy business owner. He is absolutely desperate for her, but she blatantly refused him several times. I could deduce from her character that she did not want to make mistakes she would later regret. One of them might be by having a child out of wedlock.

It was somewhat disheartening to know that the wealthy business owner was a Casanova. It was also essential to note that the Casanova was forcefully drawn toward Genevieve because of her high regard for education. Among everything that education could offer her, she also had acquired more self-discipline, which would help a man trust her. Being educated was having discipline. As important as education was, it entailed highly disciplined and accepted directions to real lives.

Many individuals who have professions who are well educated are generally well behaved members of the societies. Judging from the ways they portray their images,real lives are worth living. Many educated persons do not put themselves in danger of what would ruin their health and if they remain in strong faith, they are generally long lived. Most educated professionals do not smoke or do drugs. Anything that may be a threat to their professions is not condoned. Smoking and doing drugs can cause cancer, heart failure and numerous diseases. And the above factors can shorten a person's life. Evidently, an educated person becomes so exposed to an advanced knowledge, hence he is able to understand what is right and wrong.

Chapter Seven

When one acquires good education and stayed in a good position of authority, one became influential. This is part of the reasons some intelligent graduates attained the level of master's to a doctorate. From there, they also obtained more positions and promotions, power, respect, and even much more in their respective companies. Not to misunderstand the facts, an educated person learned and acquired knowledge, while an uneducated person chose to remain stagnant. By choosing to learn from knowledgeable or educated teachers in schools, you would enhance your understanding. But note: Learning was not limited to schools. There were other areas of discipline where learning was conveyed. However, in it all, through education, more profitable rewards were noted. Most professors, as a result of their advancement were able to breed many successful persons. Someone once said,

"An uneducated person is like a blind person."Although there were ways some individuals had dodged having an education, in the long run, it was not advantageous. This might be, for example, doing hard labor, and in the end, it shortened the person's life.

The earlier the better. Learning how to read and write should have been taught to children while they were still very young. As essential as education was, a newborn child who knew nothing at all grew up to the age of a toddler until preschool. Even yet, at this time, he/she could usually nod his/her head, especially when he/she heard from his/her parents. Taking a young kid to school at an early age to learn was of ultimate importance. As the years advanced, teaching him or her to write was wise. It was noticed that children learned faster at their younger ages. If reading and writing were not taught to children , they wouldn't have good educational foundations. Children started by listening to their parents and teachers on how ABCD to Z and 1234 and so on were read. Children were instructed to come to school with writing materials: pencils, pens, papers and crayons. As they learned how to write, they also learned coloring. Teachers made children assimilate by reading out aloud to them in front of the class. With continuous efforts from teaching the children, they grew up to the time when they started mastering their work on writing and reading. They acquired better vision that brightened them up. They increased in understanding and knowledge. Also, they were able to intelligently explore their environments. Yes, once a person knew how to read and write, he couldn't get lost in his ways. Knowing how to read and write, a fellow could advance in education. Definitely, higher education and completion of it could, no doubt, fetch a lucrative job.

During the years of your academic pursuit, a knowledge of literacy can make one become an author of books. There are many advantages of literacy. These do not exclude having to travel from one country to the other. Reading and writing gives you a lot of insights and vision. Note the joy in a little boy's mind as he is happy that he knows to read and write. He stood outside at the backyard of his parents' house watching a bird that perches at their window.

His enchantment is this:
Once I saw a little bird coming hop, hop, hop
So, I said little bird
Will you stop, stop, stop
As I was going to the window to say how do you do
But it shook a little tail, on the way it flew

After his happy moment, he felt satisfied inside that he could read aloud and hear himself do so. From here, one could envisage the amount of joy derived from being enlightened through education. No doubt there was sadness that accompanied having to do without learnable knowledge. Know that part of the importance of education was to help us humans to grow. It was also to increase our understanding. In addition, it helped us study and reach high reputation. With education, we could grow in our career and fulfill our dreams.

Read these following notations:
a) Education is the most powerful weapon which you can use to change the world (by Brainy John).

b) Education is the passport to the future, for tomorrow belongs to those who prepare for it today. Children need to get a high quality education, avoid violence and criminal justice system. We want them to learn not only reading and mathematics but fairness, caring, self-respect, family commitment and civic duty (by Colin Powell).

It is also interesting to note that education was a shared commitment between dedicated teachers, motivated students, and enthusiastic parents with high expectations (Bob Beauprez).

It is actually very wise to mark down how education integrate people. It even brings together strangers to become friends. A parent who has a positive expectation for a child holds him by the hand and walks or drives him to a chosen school. He walks into the office of the headmaster or headmistress. This is an authority figure he, as a parent, has not met before. However, due to the fact that the headmaster is an educated figure who earns the recognition of being in a respective position every arrangement that is necessary toward creating a better future for the child is initially made between his parent and the headmaster. At that early age, the child is registered into a school, and at this juncture, he is introduced into assigned class where he joined with new friends as his classmates. One can see the step by step it takes to bring people together to know one another. Education really creates an atmosphere of forming secondary families, and in fact, it enables a person's life to become more livable.

Chapter Eight

Surrounding our world today, there has been increasing technology. Technology has modified our ways. For many of the things man could do after acquiring education, machines were a must. It took educating interested and qualified individuals to operate complicated machines. To enable someone to read legibly, learning to use typewriters was a course offered in schools. Through the proper knowledge of computer keyboarding, a student could meet the required words per minute, which was normally forty-five (45) words per minute. During a job search, a prospective typist who reached the recommended speed could be hired. COMPUTER KNOWLEDGE: There are many complicated loopholes for understanding computers and their usage. As important as they are, it takes a knowledgeable and qualified instructor to teach or educate students about them.

Mr. Joseph Williams had enjoyed what it was like to live and be a leader. After his high school years were over, his spirit of determination for academic pursuit did not stop. Among other things he acquired from higher education, he realized the most precious advantage of him not giving up was gaining integrity, authority, respect, and a very good way that was worthy of living exemplary lives. Mr. Joseph Williams got a job in the bank. He was lucky that someone connected him to the bank with his high school completion. While he began working and making a manageable income, he registered into a polytechnic school as a part-time student. He went in for accountancy. After two years at the lower level, he submitted his credential to the bank, and his salary was increased. Then, as long as he expected to rise to the position of manager, he was blessed that he was admitted into a university. The school accepted some subjects he took at the polytechnic. So, with full-time at the University, he would not have to run it for exactly four years. So, while he continued to work, he attended lectures in the evenings. And no sooner than he knew it, he graduated as an accountant. Again, his salary was raised. He began working diligently and was effective. And one day, he was promoted to a bank manager. He was elated at this, and his salary doubled. As his work continued, he became highly connected to people of different classes. He was kind and delighted to help most customers. These people he helped recognized him and spread how good a man he was, and their impressions of him truly made him feel happier. Henceforth, whenever he encountered some people with certain expectations of him, he encouraged them to value education. He told them he did not know where he would have been if he had not been determined to be well educated.

As the year went by, while Mr. Joseph Williams was still working in the bank, he noticed that the chief executive officer of the bank had a few years to retire. The bank now decided to send him abroad to study for the office and a master's degree. He furthered the course in a university in Britain. After the completion, the position and seat of a CEO were already waiting for him in the bank. His joy was utmost with a higher increase in his salary. Not only did Joseph have an income increase, but with connections to people inside and out, he won a great reputation, integrity, and power.

I can still recall how my brother, Ngezelonye Victor Ugezene, won a coat of strong personality and dignity. Although he is late now, however, his advancement during his lifetime had many attributes with being highly intelligent and having an education. With his kind of intelligence, his mates saw him as a genius. He always came out in first positions in schools. So, through the years of elementary school to the University where he studied civil engineering, he continued to maintain top positions. He graduated with first-class honors. When Victor was admitted into the University, the Board of Education published his name in the national newspaper, and he received awards because of his high score. This gave him great joy and the light to see that education was advantageous and important. To him, having opportunities and hope became the norm for advancement and betterment.

With education, the world and its environment remain a better place. With development, our surroundings become habitable. It is easier for connections to remind us of things about life. Cars, airplanes, boats, ships, etc., continue to be manufactured. Transportation continues to be accessible. Among other ways to prepare for living, education surfaces as the most preferred way. With all that education has, it is difficult for some people. No doubt it takes a lot of challenges to learn, but in the final run, it is worth it.

Chapter Nine

It may seem rather exhausting having enlarged and elaborated on the advantages of education. It is still interesting to learn further about it. It is discovered that once a learned person receives his/her educational qualification and obtains an employable position, for example, a teacher, he/she then conveys his/her knowledge to students. From then on, he/she prepares the younger generation for a promising future. The preparation usually will carry them on. They can become painstaking and fight the spirit of laziness, which brings failure, delay, and procrastination. Once these bad attributes set in, the aftereffects of a good life come to a halt. Sometimes, the result is: *had I known.*

It is really amazing to see the positive results and benefits of an educated person. With the right mind focused on elements of discipline, which are already embedded in an educated person, he is never likely to fail. One can see how lovable and acceptable an educated literate is, especially to children who want to emulate him or her.

There are these two children of two different families. They are absolutely from poor backgrounds. The poor parents of Adam Fieldflock, as the name of one child was called, tried so hard to start him in elementary education. Since they could not feed him three meals a day, they struggled so hard to pay his school levy and buy books. Mr. and Mrs. Fieldflock earned their living by working hard for farmers. Sometimes, some of them would cruelly choose to use them without paying, and both would cry, to no avail.

Mr. Fieldflock's son, Adam, began elementary education at seven years instead of five years. The cause of it resulted from poverty. The poor little boy was a special blessing to his parents. Some days after school, when he had finished his homework, he would go to a Catholic church parishioner's house. He would be on his knees and ask him to pray for his parents and him. At nine years, he became baptized after attending six months of catechism. He kept attending church every Sunday. He usually listened to preachers and learned to pray. Besides the church services, he chose about three days a week to go to the open market to help his parents sell vegetables and melons. This then added extra money to his parents' hands.

Adam did excellently well at school. He usually came out second in position out of forty members in a class. When he reached his final year at school, he was not bold enough to tell his parents that he would like to attend secondary or high school. He thought that even if they might like the idea, the money might not be available for further education. As Adam's fate had it, before his final year, the school headmaster selected him to represent his school in a writing contest. It was a national presentation. He had very good, sound, legible handwriting. Among the four selected students in four different schools in the state, Adam was the only one whose handwriting was outstanding and he was chosen as the winner of the contest. From this good deed by God, he was offered financial aid and a scholarship. The awards were not only seeing him through secondary school but also through his university education. It was a unique offer that elated him. Finally, he completed elementary school and passed the subsequent examination that led him to high school. No sooner than he knew it, his high school education was over.

He got admitted to study pharmacy at the University. After his university education, he was employed at a pharmaceutical company. He worked diligently well and earned a good income. With all that he became, he built a house for his parents, and he was sending them good sums of money every month. He also married a medical doctor who related to him with respect, love, caring, and appreciation. They were happy and blessed with four children. From this instance, one can fancy and view the value of education.

The other family, Mr. and Mrs. Golden Fox, who was also very poor, found it difficult to sustain themselves. Their only son grew up to be such a stubborn and cruel boy and very senseless. Both parents had a well-to-do uncle who wanted to help the boy, Max Fox, as his name is called, but he was defiant. He refused to go to school, and each time he saw his uncle coming to visit and encourage him, he would run away.

Max grew up to be twenty-five years and never thought of something to do to help himself and his parents. He did not care about anybody. He did not want to be inspired. Now and then, especially when there was nothing to eat, he would beat both parents. He could not even consider that they were not staying in a house of their own. They were only occupying one small bedroom in their relative's house. Their lives continued to go from poverty to illness. One day, Max's father, Golden, died and his wife became very sick after grieving. The worst part was that her son, Max, who could not get an education, still beat her. Later, his relative, in whose house they were living, could not handle Max's behavior and asked them to move out. The poor lady was pushed outside, and she became homeless where she died.

Readers, you can see the consequences of not having an education.

Chapter Ten

Education has brought productive and tangible rewards. It also creates motivation and a sense of practice in you. It is said, "Practice makes perfect."By educating many interested individuals, life has become easier to live. An educated woman who is single either by no marriage or by divorce can support herself. With her qualification, she can adhere to hope and wait until she can get a job. While searching for the job, she is not heartbroken because she has a certificate. Read some of these quotes:

1) "An investment in knowledge pays the best interest."(Benjamin Franklin).

2) "Education is not only preparation for life; education is life itself."(John Denvey).

3) "The roots of education are bitter, but the fruit is sweet."(Aristotle)

The advantages that education has for interested students should not be overlooked. In many countries, the consequences or penalties someone who refuses or shows little or no interest in schooling has to face are under rules and laws. A school truant can be like a child who dodges school attendance. During the waking hours when he is to get himself ready for school the way his parent prepares him to, he prefers to hide away and miss class lessons.

When he even leaves and gets to the school premises, he deviates and goes to another place. Then, after the classes are over, he comes back home to eat and lie to his parents. He might continue with being absent from classes until it catches up with him. With such an unpalatable behavior, at the end of the school year, he will have to show his parents his poor report cards. Usually, he might get the report that he is expelled from school. So, in an apparent notice, the journey of an unforeseen future and circumstance begins.

It will be interesting to appreciate and ponder on what is happening in the world of an educated professional, especially among medical doctors, pharmacists, medical laboratory technologists, etc. Many patients struggle with sickness and are close to death. It takes doctors to cure them and restore them to life. Through the intensive training that doctors have undergone in their different disciplines, their abilities to treat patients are sure. Readers, I recommend you research and know the various specialties in the field of medicine.

Pharmacists manufacture medications to treat the sick ones. By being educated, a pharmacist can process natural herbs and leaves into tablets, pills, or medications of different brands and generics. Many of the manufactured medications are lifesavers. They can make patients or consumers live longer.

Medical technologists do the testing of patients' health conditions through the channel of technological equipment in the laboratories. The process helps doctors to diagnose a patient. This enables physicians to give patients faster and more effective treatments for their diseases.

It is not wise to neglect the fact that those who aim toward a higher level in school do so because of their passing grades. These are usually grades of A's or B's or C's, or notably advancing toward 100 percent. Individuals who cannot make passing grades are dropped out of school, and it creates a feeling of despair and a threat to future success. A study from biological science has some notable facts about why some persons are more intelligent than others. These more intelligent individuals have genetic traits that help them understand and assimilate given courses or subjects better. The gene is a hereditary character from a father, mother,or both parents.

Engineering professionals are students who received their engineering degree from the study of engineering. It takes very intelligent students to be in the field. Civil engineers make good money and some of them receive construction contracts of various types. They build bridges, government projects, houses, schools, and companies. Electrical engineers construct electricity. Other engineers see to their respective interests and disciplines.

Through learning or being educated, some advanced educators pass to learners the usefulness of physical education. Physical fitness is a key component of a healthy lifestyle. Physical activities are needed to assist in the absorption of nutrients in the body. It improves cardiovascular strength. It helps with blood circulation and conveys a significant impact in pumping blood to the entire body. For younger children in school to stimulate their bodies to the benefits of physical education (PE) this poem is written:

POEM:

1, 2 buckle my shoe

3, 4 knock at the door

5, 6 pick-up sticks

7, 8 lay them straight

9, 10 A big fat hen

It really takes putting their bodies and acting on the words of the poem, and they definitely are relieved from tightness. Starting even with physical education in elementary or primary school, activities are an important role in the healthy growth and development of bones and cartilages. An exercise like jumping is very important for school children as this activity produces a force onto the bone that enhances its strength and growth. So now it becomes understandable that PE is a part of education taught in schools.

Education has brought ideas of reading, writing, books, newspapers, magazines, technologies, travel, transportation, etc., into play. It is essential to touch on why books are important to students, among all they have to understand about education. Books are guides: compared to computer usage, books are readily portable and last longer. Reading books teaches one to focus and concentrate on one thing at a time.

Yes, it is difficult to have a head start with getting into a school and beginning your education. However, once you put your interest, mind, and faith in it, something good comes out of it. It is absolutely necessary to heed the saying, "Make hay while the sun shines. . ."

Chapter Eleven

Take time and read the thesis by Kafoumba Alfred, an accomplished professional who appreciates his days of schooling. He states why education is so important in our life. When he started thinking about why education is very important, he remembered his high school years when he used to spend almost five hours on mathematics homework. He usually woke up at 6:00 a.m. and got ready for his PSAL soccer game after school. He recalled his teachers' subjects, his studies, and the fun. He never really hated school, but Kafoumba had seen many of his peers who hated going to school. He had some friends who did not like the idea of studying. Some needed to be in summer school recovery. He was always focused because he wanted to become a software engineer. He knew it would be hard and very challenging. However, he believed he could handle the challenge. You can perceive that the first thing that struck Kafoumba was knowledge.

Education gives humans knowledge of the world around them and changes it into something better. It develops in us a perspective of looking at life. It helps us build opinions and have points of view on things in life. People debate over the subject of whether education is the only thing that gives knowledge. Some say education is the process of gaining information about the surrounding world, while knowledge is something different. They might be right, but then again, information cannot be converted into knowledge without education. Education makes us capable of interpreting things, among other things. It is not just about lessons in textbooks. It is also about the lessons of life.

Having good education promotes a genuine sense of self-appreciation. Also, it exposes awareness of how the community of one's dwelling takes one. Furthermore, schooling and the accomplishments that follow it broaden our horizons. It takes you the extra miles. Part of the numerous advantages of having an education does not rule out its ability to take a successful and intelligent student to places in the world he does not know he would ever be. If a student continues to perform very intelligently, sometimes his school deems it necessary to send him abroad on a scholarship. Schools like Oxford University, Cambridge University, and Harvard University have been known to receive highly or well-performed students on sponsorship curricula. Having to go to another place gives you the light to what is happening in a different world. It also exposes one to people of different cultures. With education, a student comes to learn a new culture and new perspectives in life. It further teaches the student how to adapt and mingle. There is an instance where education takes you as far as naturalizing as a citizen of another country. And this actually brings the idea of dual citizenship.

Education not only progresses the learner but also classifies people according to their methods of their living. It enhances high self-esteem, prestige, and acceptability. Schooling for learners to have education or better perspectives is a possibility. However, to some, it is not an easy task just as mentioned earlier. Some wise ones resolve to this saying: "When the going gets tough, the tough get going." I believe the days and times are still fresh when the preparations to get admitted into a school of your choice are done by testing. Depending on your score, you might be accepted to enroll in some classes. In this instance, you might be placed in classes depending on how low or high your score is. This is why some students are required to do prerequisites to prepare them for the core-requisites classes.

It is also important to touch on the matter of juvenile delinquency. JUVENILE DELINQUENCY can be controlled or eradicated by having a proper and good education. By stopping juvenile delinquency, children grow up to become disciplined citizens of their countries, and there will be no need to commit crimes. The eradication of juvenile delinquency helps to stop school truancy among youths particularly.

In addition, working and earning income makes life worth living. Having to combine working and schooling is a possibility, once the focus and concentration are there. It is absolutely essential not to waste your youthful ages."Early to bed, early to rise."Just from the onset of the rising sun, make yourself ready. ABC and 123, a child counts at the early stage of his life. Children are more ready to learn virtually anything at an early age. It might seem rather redundant making this statement, but believe me, early to bed, early to rise isn't bed in the literal sense but true readiness to life. Surprisingly, some have eluded a real preparedness for life. It is very important and should be given serious attention. Note this poem:

Poem:

When Jick and Jack went to School, maybe Jick is the lazy one

When Jick and Jack went to school, maybe Jick is the lazy one

Jack is up earlier and ready to go

However, Jick takes extra time and stretches reluctantly.

It is not out of place to wear a coat of an exemplary life. Better emulate it. Mondays through Fridays, wake up and be productive instead of staying stagnant.

Hello readers and interested individuals of this book, make sure to understand that part of my objectives as the author is to entail a sense of focus. So please, if anyone lacks interest in achievement, just change that attitude. I bet you are better off happier in life than living with regrets.

Kiki has actually used her sense of realization and is able to correct the mistakes she made at the early age of her life. If she had lazily adapted to the unpleasant habits , it would have resulted to such a devastating situations to her future.

It is essential to know that the lessons this book is teaching do not only apply to Kiki's life but also to anyone else concerned. Even with matters of education, there is no boundary. Sometimes, this quote goes with it: " It is better to be late than never."There is no age limit."Once there is life, there is hope."If you were not able to go to school during your younger years, an Adult Education can fit you in.

Virtue!

Believe in God.

Have hope and determination.

Have self-confidence and self-motivation.

Plan and set your goals.

Pursue those goals with faith and confidence.

www.ingramcontent.com/pod-product-compliance
Lightning Source LLC
Chambersburg PA
CBHW070921250626

47159CB00014B/2292